IT'S BEGINNING TO LOOK A LOT LIKE LOVE

A Novella

L.M. Maretti

CONTENTS

Chapter One

Ember

I watch my bags roll through airport security. It's been about eighteen months since I last visited Silver Springs.

"Here you are, ma'am, you're all set."

Thanking airport security, I make my way to the loading dock. If the impending snowstorm doesn't cause delays, my flight should be leaving in an hour.

I was tempted to tell my parents and younger sister, Aspen, that I wouldn't be coming home this year. I've never felt less Christmassy in my entire life. But I knew my family would be heartbroken, and after the week I've had, I needed to see some familiar faces.

The stock market decided to throw a tantrum. The company I worked for was going under, leaving everyone, me included, jobless in the week before Christmas. My world turned upside down overnight.

My job had been the only thing tying me to Boston. In the three years I'd been in this city, I had worked my ass off, leaving no time for a social life or making any connections, besides a few random dates here and there. Ironically, without a job, I'll have plenty of time for a social life—I'll just be homeless because I won't be able to afford my rent. I pay forty-two hundred dollars for my one bedroom. I can't even get a roommate. Jesus, I need a drink. I check my watch deciding

I have time before my flight and walk towards the sounds of music, clanging dishes, and people. Glancing up, I snort to myself - *Harpoon Brewery*. Might as well get in the spirit of my trip back home to good old Tennessee. Yee-fuckity-haw.

"What can I get you?" the bartender asks as I sit down on one of the tall stools at the bar.

"I'll take a mug of your best beer." I pull my long red hair up into a bun and take off my gray pea coat.

"A woman who likes a good beer," a rich deep voice remarks next to me. "Sexy," the guy winks. "Better than those sugary mixed drinks most of the ladies order." He must be at least fifty-five with salt and pepper hair. A good solid build and a jawline that resembles a movie star. He's got that hot older man thing going for him, however, the last thing I need right now is a hook up to fuck up my head before I board a plane to the town that has already given me plenty of emotional baggage.

"Glad you approve of my drink choice," I respond dryly, pulling out my phone as I feel it vibrate in my pocket. I read a text from my sister.

Ember, please, for the love of God, get here now! Mom's bitching at dad about everything and dad's walking around grumbling.

So, no different than any other day?

Exactly. When does your flight leave?

In an hour, if the snow cooperates. But I have a layover in Chicago.

Ugh, I don't know if I'll make it that long. Mom just burnt the cookies in the oven and is running around opening all the windows and doors swearing like a sailor. Dad is making excuses as to why he must run to the hardware store.

I chuckle, picturing it all clearly.

He always was a smart man; you should find your own excuse to escape for a while.

The sound of the stool next to me makes a scraping sound as someone else settles down, "This seat taken?" a deep voice rumbles.

"Please help yourself," I respond, watching him glance at me from head to toe and back, stopping at my cleavage peeking out of my green Christmas sweater.

I'm sitting between two guys currently eye fucking me while I drink a watered-down beer in a crowded airport. My life is no better than yours at this point.

That's awkward, unless they're hot. Oh!!!! Then do both so you can tell me all the details, but please don't miss your flight!!! :(:(:(

I glance up at the guy who just sat down, noticing that his eyes are clearly focused on my double D's. I then look back over to the first man, who's doing the same, and roll my eyes in response.

I'd say the opportunity is there, but I'm not feeling it.

Bummer. FYI, I saw you know who at the grocery store the other day..........

Don't start, we're just friends!

Who's starting? I'm just saying. He asked if you were coming in for a visit.

I hope you lied!!!!!! I can't see him, it's too complicated!

Well........

Aspen Marie Riley!!!!!!

What! He gave me those puppy dog eyes, and then, he licked his bottom lip. You shouldn't have told me what his tongue is capable of!

My thighs clench at the visual of Garrett Hayes' soft pink tongue swiping across his plump bottom lip after the one time our friendship had crossed the line, and his head had ended up between my legs. I may have been drunk at that New year's party, but I remember every second of his talented mouth on my puss- I swipe my hand over my face and slide my phone back into the pocket of my black jeans with a sigh. I do not need to be stirring up sex dreams about Garrett Hayes again. The last time I let myself go there, I woke up with wet panties for weeks.

Chapter Two

Ember

The flight to Chicago turned out to be uneventful. As I sit in O'Hare International Airport waiting for my next plane, I watch the people around me. Two days before Christmas and the place is jam packed. Families scrambling to make their flights, parents looking frantic, little kids screaming, teenagers looking bored down at their cell phones.

Growing up, we didn't travel much. My parents grew up in Silver Springs and are high school sweethearts. I always wondered why they didn't want to explore the world more, but they seem content to stay in the little town where everyone knows everyone's business.

I've always been the oddball in my family. I grew up wanting to explore everything. My mom said that was why I walked before I could crawl. I was eager to go the minute I was born.

I guess that's why when I started to fall hard for Garrett Hayes the summer after my senior year of college, I felt like I had to rein myself in. If I let a man stop me from pursuing my dreams, I was going to be fucked. We had been strictly platonic, just friends. I hadn't intended on falling for him, but any woman would. He was arguably one of the most handsome men I'd ever seen. The kind that belongs on the cover of a magazine instead of some Ho bunk town in Tennessee. He was tall, had dark hair and blue eyes and to top it off, incredibly charming. When we met through mutual friends, we just clicked. What started as us hanging out together in groups, eventually led to just the two of us. There was an ease about hanging out with Garrett. He enjoyed sharing the luxuries his family could provide- things I'd never experienced before. I got caught up in the excitement of it. We went sailing on their yacht, drove fancy convertibles around the countryside, and ate at all sorts of upscale restaurants. He even convinced me to try escargot!

But even as I started to fall for Garrett, I kept my goal of independence in mind - applying to jobs and never losing focus on achieving my career ambitions. When a company offered me the job of my dreams in Boston, it was a bittersweet moment; I accepted it knowing that our relationship would end when I moved away.

We send the occasional text or goofy selfie, he sends me flowers for my birthday and calls me late at night when he's had a few too many drinks. Other than that, we've moved on. Our lives are different now. He's busy learning the ropes of his family business, and I'm- well I *was* busy with my job in Boston.

Do I often wonder what life would've been like had I stayed in Silver Springs, or we'd tried being more than friends? Of course, I do, but in the end, I know I made the wise choice. I'm not a woman who would be happy being a Stepford wife. I want adventures, to make my own money, I like being an independent woman. Up until recently, I'd been doing well at it. I climbed the corporate ladder, becoming one of the most successful businesswomen in my field.

Things were as they were meant to be. My inner monologue is interrupted by the loudspeaker-

"Ladies and gentlemen, we regret to inform you that due to inclement weather conditions, flight AA345 from Chicago O'Hare International Airport to Nashville International Airport has been canceled. We

apologize for any inconvenience this may cause. Please proceed to the airline's customer service desk for assistance with rebooking or further information. Thank you for your understanding."

Chapter Three

Ember

I listen to my mother's sobs through the phone line that have been going on for the last twenty minutes as I rub my temples.

"It's just not going to feel like Christmas! Why bother going ahead with the holiday at all if we can't be together!" she wails while I stand in the middle of the airport surrounded by people having their own similar crisis.

"Mom, you still have Aspen and dad there, the three of you can enjoy the holiday, and I'll be back home as soon as I can," I try to reason.

"Marge, give me the phone," I hear my father's gruff voice in the background. After a few more sobs and my father's stern voice, she reluctantly hands over the phone.

"Hey sugar plum." Tears prick at my eyelids as soon as my dad greets me by the nickname he gave me as a little girl.

"Hey dad," I sigh, suddenly feeling mentally and physically exhausted. "What a mess, huh?"

"I'll say," He sighs heavily. "Your mom will be fine once she calms down. What is your plan until they open flights again?"

My chest tightens with dread at his question, and my eyes dart around at all the frantic people surrounding me most likely trying to figure out the same thing.

"Well, I'm going to have to find a hotel room," I say hopelessly.

My father sighs again, "Alright, well, start on that, and call us back to let us know, love you."

My throat closes up and tears fill my eyes. "Love you too dad," I choke out before ending the call.

Tears stream down my face as I sink deeper into a corner of the airport. Being an adult has never seemed so difficult. I lean against the wall and take out my phone to search for somewhere to stay for the night. Everywhere is booked and each call increases my feeling of dread and loneliness.

I hesitantly pick up the phone and press it to my ear, crossing my fingers, my legs, and my eyes, as I make the last phone call.

"Whispering Pines Pint-Sized Haven, where even the squirrels envy our square footage, how can I help you?"

"Hello," my voice quivers," do you have any vacancies and please, please say yes" I beg.

"Oh sweetheart," the woman's sugary voice croons through the line. "Let me check our availability. Charlie!" she yells suddenly, making me jump, her tone drastically changing to one of urgency. I hear mumbling in the background before she returns with more softened tones into the receiver. "Yes dear, we do have one vacancy left. What's your name?"

A relieved sigh escapes my lips as I utter a pitiful "Oh thank God. My name is Ember. Ember Riley, and I'll be there to check in as soon as I can find a taxi, Uber, horse and sleigh, or whatever I have to, to get there."

***

I stumble through the thick snow like a lost yeti, desperately seeking refuge. The flickering porch light beckons like a beacon of hope on the tiny cabin. The Uber driver got stuck in a snowbank at the bottom of the hill, leaving me no choice but to trudge the rest of the way on foot. My suitcase's wheels are so caked with snow that they've transformed into the equivalent of two giant snowballs rolling alongside me. When I finally reach the small cabin set back in the woods, I open the creaky door, and am greeted by the scent of wood and a tiny crackling fireplace. The mismatched furniture and worn rugs give the place a comforting charm. Though the cabin might be not much larger than the size of a shoe box and a bit weathered, in this moment, it feels as if I've stepped into the Taj Mahal.

I set my suitcase on the floor and lay back on a patchwork quilt spread on the bed letting out a long shuddering breath. I'm out of tears, I cried so much in the Uber on the way here I scared the poor driver. Tomorrow morning is Christmas Eve. By the looks of it, the weather won't clear up for a few days. I'll be all alone for Christmas.

I wish I was twelve again, when things were simple. My biggest concern was if Tommy Tunis was going to pick on me about my braces and red hair. In those days, Christmas Eve was full of excitement and anticipation. Now it's just another day trying to survive with nothing but my thoughts and the snowstorm outside.

Chapter Four

Ember

When I arrived at Whispering Pines, the *pint-sized haven* owned by Sue and Charles Clearwater, they welcomed me with open arms. They even extended an invitation to their Christmas Eve meal. As I stumbled into the lobby last night, covered in snow, I must have looked as pitiful as I felt—eyes swollen from crying, cheeks red from the cold December night air, and my rolling suitcase transformed into a solid block of snow and ice.

Sue, with her thick white hair cascading down her shoulders and full warm cheeks, and Charlie, with his kind eyes, hinted that Sue was an excellent cook by patting his stomach. I was grateful for their kindness; I had endured enough emotional bashing for one day.

What I need this morning is a good hot shower. I set the water temperature to just below scalding and step in, hoping it will wash away some stress. My shoulders feel like they're nothing but one solid knot. As the hot water rushes over me, I try to clear my mind, but it's no use.

Why does life have to be so damn hard? I'm not ready to find a new job, I liked the one I had, I was comfortable there. The people were kind. The few dates I had gone on with guys I'd found on Tinder weren't anything to write home about but at least I was making an effort to have a social life. I force myself out of the shower and dry off, staring blankly at myself in the foggy mirror.

I need Starbucks and Panera. If Door Dash could even make it through snow, I doubt they would deliver out this far. The tiny cabin echoes with the familiar chorus of The Office theme song, as my sister's signature ringtone chimes in. I promised her we would facetime this afternoon, with a groan I throw myself across the bed and grab my cell of the nightstand.

"Do you have it on?" Aspen screeches excitedly as I answer.

"Do I have what on?" I ask, knowing perfectly well what she's referring to.

"Come on, Ember," she whines in the most Aspen way possible, "it's bad enough you're missing our annual tradition-"

"We've been to their holiday party once, that's not annual."

"Well, it's going to be! And I worked hard picking out these outfits, so try it on and call me back!"

***

Exactly ten minutes later a familiar theme song plays again.

"I'm trying to do the belt;" I pant and squirm pushing my boobs into the white fluffy corset until they threaten to spill over and then buckle the wide black belt while I stand in front of the bathroom mirror. "I feel like an idiot Aspen. The red skirt barely covers my ass!"

"Why is it taking you so long?" she shouts through the phone, to which I huff, "because my tits and ass are two sizes larger than yours!" I blow a lock of sweaty red hair off my forehead, my cheeks flushed from the exertion of trying to get in the damn thing. "Why did you get us the same size?"

"You said you wanted to be slutty Santa, it was either that or a slutty elf!"

"Well, this is it, " I hold up the phone towards the full-length mirror so she can see, "I look like a busted can of biscuits. Thank God I did get snowed it. There's no way I would've gone to the Hannigans party wearing this thing."

"Fuck that! You look hot!"

"Ppff! right!" I snort "You just got me this one so I'd look awful, and the guys would go for

you instead of me at the party!" I accuse just as a loud knock rattles the door causing me to jump.

"Who's that?" my sister asks.

I roll my eyes, thoroughly annoyed, "How would I know? I haven't answered the door!"

"You're so grumpy! I'm not the one who created the snow, Ember! I'm not the one who canceled the flight and I'm not-"

"I'm not grumpy!" I shout back into the phone, "You're just annoying!"

The knock comes louder, interrupting our spat.

My sister huffs loudly into the phone, "Are you going to answer it? Or let the person just stand out there? Sometimes I wonder if you think about anyone else at all!"

The knock grows louder still as I toss my phone/sister on the bed and wretch open the door with a whoosh.

Chapter Five

Ember

I blink rapidly at the stunningly handsome figure before me. I squint against the sun that plays hopscotch on the snow outside, causing a halo to surround him. It was like the man had his own personal spotlight, and I half-expected a choir of heavenly voices to burst into a rendition of "Hark the Herald Angels Sing!"

I rub at my eyes, it's this damned Santa costume! It constricted my airway and I'm having legit hallucinations. Pfft! and *I'm* the sister who doesn't think of others. But Aspen can go around cutting off people's airways and that's okay. No one cares. Just like when she was horrible all year, and mom and dad said there was no way she was getting a Barbie dream house. What was right dead center under the tree on Christmas morning? A fuckin' Barbie dreamhouse. Because Aspen can do whatever she wants, and everyone is fine-

"Ember?" Great! Now the hallucinations are speaking to me!

"Ember?" It repeats as a large gust of freezing frigid wind rips through the air causing my skin to break out in goosebumps and my brain to come back to reality. Wait, what?

"Garrett?"

"Hey?" He leans against the door frame with a sly grin, "it was one hell of a trip," he eyes me up and down, "but man, am I glad I made it."

My breath hitches, "What are you doing here?" I look behind him, seeing he's alone. "How did you get here and why? I'm so confused" My teeth chatter as another cold burst of wind billows through the doorway.

A low chuckle comes from his chest, "let me in, and I'll explain."

"Oh God! Yes, sorry, you must be freezing! Come in!" I usher.

"DID YOU SAY GARRETT HAYES IS AT THE DOOR?" Aspen's voice echoes through the cabin. "OH MY GOD, AND YOU WERE JUST SAYING-"

"I'll call you back," I hit end. And look over at Garrett, in what I can only imagine, is a look of utter embarrassment, confusion, and shock.

He shrugs, his voice soft, "I saw your dad at the hardware store, he said you got snowed in and would be alone on Christmas."

I suck in a breath, "You drove all this way?"

"It only took about eight hours;" he shrugs again like it's nothing. "It was well worth it to see the look on your face," he reaches out, running the back of his finger over my pink cheek and along my jawline. His eyes travel down my body, "and this get up you've got on." He wiggles his eyebrows at me.

I jump back, "EEK!" I squeal, yanking the quilt off the bed to cover myself. "It's Aspen's fault!"

"Remind me to thank her," he smirks and then his tongue peeks out as he licks across his bottom lip.

I swear the heat spreads from the tips of my toes to right between my thighs. "Um, I'll be right back." I dash to the bathroom.

My heart thuds out of my chest as I peel the Santa costume off my body and rip open my suitcase. Garrett came all this way to see me?

I'm not prepared for this; I don't even have anything cute to wear. Wait. Where the fuck is he going to sleep? Oh my God, I'm going to be sick. I didn't shave my legs. In my defense, it's cold, and they provide a small amount of warmth. I'm lying, I'm lazy, and no one sees them anyway. I run a brush through my hair and pile it on my head. My wardrobe consists of pajamas, jeans, and tacky Christmas sweaters. The only place I was intending on going was the Hannigans party, the rest of the time, I planned to stay in my pjs and wallow in my sorrows!

"Are you going to hide in the bathroom the whole time I'm here?" his deep voice rumbles through the door.

"Coming right out!" I holler back as I settle on my nicest set of flannel pajama bottoms and a white tank top.

Chapter Six

Garrett

I didn't think it could be possible, but Ember is more stunning than I remember. Her long, thick red hair flows down her back, and her wide, piercing blue eyes stare back at me. I thought I had developed frostbite on ninety percent of my body after my car got stuck at the bottom of the hill, and I had to trudge up here to find her cabin. But when she opened that door dressed as Santa Claus, her breasts spilling out of her top — well, let's just say the cold wasn't a problem for one essential part of my body. It stood at attention like a mighty soldier.

I'm warming myself by the fireplace while I pull out my cell and send a text to my younger sister, Sutton.

I made it

Thank God. Was she surprised?

That's an understatement

I didn't know you were such a romantic......
Garrett and Ember sitting in a tree KISSING...

Shut up brat lol

You're really into her huh?

We have this thing, I don't know, it's hard to explain. But when her dad told me what happened, I couldn't not come and who knows? You can't win if you don't try! How are you doing?

I'll fill you in when you get home! Merry Christmas, stud. Go get em'!

I can feel the warmth coming back in my fingers and toes when Ember finally steps out of the bathroom. Her cheeks are flushed, and she's piled her hair on top of her neck showing off the skin on her neck. The neck I'm dying to taste. I'm disappointed to see the costume is gone but not for long when I see it's been replaced by pajama bottoms that she looks more comfortable in and a white tank top that I can see the outline of her nipples in. Down mighty soldier.

"Hey" her voice is soft as she sits down on the edge of the small love seat that faces the fireplace.

"Hey" I can't help the giant dorky grin that spreads across my face. "It's been a while" I take a seat next to her.

"Three years" we both say at the same time and then laugh awkwardly. My palms are now sweating, and I run them down my thighs. Okay, buck up, Garrett. You've been waiting for your second chance with this girl, you came all this way. Don't be a fuckin' pansy ass.

"Want a drink?" she asks, rising suddenly and heading towards the small refrigerator.

"That would be amazing," I breathe running my hands through my hair, the swag I usually have with women goes right out the fuckin' window when it comes to Ember. It always has. In spite of the fact that we were mostly in the friend zone, I had the time of my life with her that summer three years ago.

"I doubt it's nearly as nice as the wines you have at the fancy smancy Hayes manor," she hands me a holiday mug filled to the brim. "But it will have to do, I pleaded with my Uber driver to stop at a gas station so I could at least have a bottle of wine to drown my sorrows in."

"It's not bad," With an audible gulp, I force the liquid down my throat and try to hide my cough behind my hand.

Ember throws her head back with a laugh, "You're such a liar!" and then takes a large gulp wincing as it goes down. "Okay, it's awful," she coughs.

"I was trying to be polite;" I chuckle, gulping the rest down in one go, hoping it would give me a bit of liquid courage. The taste is a blend of evergreen and gasoline, like licking the floor of a mechanic's garage. I look over at her, and our eyes meet as we both say “pine and gasoline” in unison and then erupt in laughter. I love the way the corners of her eyes crinkle and the bright gold flakes in her blue irises shine when she laughs. Ember doesn't have one of those small delicate, unsure laughs. She laughs with her entire body, loud and brassy. It's infectious.

"I still can't believe you're here," she whispers as her laughter dies down, her delicate hands gripping her glass as she swirls the last drop before refilling our cups.

"It's what friends do, right?" Her sparkling blues meet mine.

"Yeah," Her lips pull into a smile, "I guess they do."

"So," I lean back against the plush cushions, "tell me about the wild city of Boston."

Chapter Seven

Ember

The fire crackles in the fireplace, the bottle of wine empty between us. I lean into the cushy loveseat, my muscles relaxed from the alcohol. Garrett sits next to me, his body warm and inviting. The smell of his cologne, mixed with wood smoke from the fire, is heavenly.

"It sounds like you had it good for a while," he says, arms crossed over his broad chest as he stares into the flames. "Were you happy there?"

I take a moment to consider his question before answering. "At first, yeah. It was exciting, but also exhausting. Between work, I didn't have any time for myself or to explore the city I was so pumped about living in. I spent all day in a dark office staring at a computer."

"Like my father and brother," he nods, eyebrows furrowing. "I know what that's like. That's why I'm struggling to become a partner at Hayes Enterprises: I don't want to be stuck in an office all day, but I do want success."

"Exactly, so we just need to determine our own definition of success." I curl my legs beneath me and prop an elbow on the back of the loveseat to face Garrett.

He shifted, leaning in, his warm brown eyes intense and focused on me. Tucking a strand of hair behind my ear with a gentle touch, his voice turned soft and raspy, "If it's a job you want, firecracker, Hayes Enterprises is always hiring, and I've got some pretty good connections." A grin tugged at his lips.

I knew that if I stayed in tiny Silver Springs, seeing the same people day in and day out would only lead to more of the same. But could I find whatever I was searching for in Boston? That was the question.

"That's very kind of you." His grin faltered, so I took his large hand in mine. "I need to make my own way, Garrett. I'm not going to find what I'm looking for in little Silver Springs, Tennessee," I added with a slight chuckle, watching the light in his eyes dim.

"Right," he nodded. "Yeah, it was just a suggestion." He stood, heading toward the kitchenette. "What are we going to eat? I'm starving."

We say nothing as I watch him move around the tiny room opening cabinets. Maybe it's the alcohol causing things to get so heavy in the room, maybe it is the things that were left unsaid so many years ago. I follow after him, guilt gnawing away at my insides. I get too blunt when I drink. Aspen always says I lose my filter and act like my mother.

I take a deep breath. "Garrett, you know I'm grateful for your friendship, I care about you very much," I say softly trying to find the right words to say, "But I want to explore a world bigger than Silver Springs."

"You don't need to explain," he shakes his head, leaning his hip against the counter. "I've always been shit at expressing my feelings," he sighs.

"Your sense of adventure is one of the things I like most about you." He runs his fingers through his hair, taking a deep breath. "But being here with you, like this, it just feels right.

And-well, I guess I just wish I could fit in your life somewhere," he put his hands in the pockets of his jeans, his rugged features softening in the glow of the fire.

"You do," I walk closer, looking up at him.

His warm eyes search mine; I feel a flutter in my chest, "As more than a friend, Ember."

CHAPTER EIGHT

EMBER

"More?" I hear the words leave my mouth.

He searches my eyes, "You don't feel it?"

"I-" I do. I always have, but how?

"Listen," he holds up his hands, "I shouldn't have just said it like that. It's the cheap wine," he chuckles awkwardly, his cheeks turning pink. "Let's just enjoy our time together." He scratches the back of his neck, his bicep stretching the sleeve of his henley.

The brisk jingle of the phone attached to the wall interrupts us, followed by metallic chimes that echo through the cabin. "Well, that's a first," Garrett chuckles. "Never heard one of those before."

I hesitantly pick up the heavy pale-yellow receiver, "Hello?" Garret and my eyes stay locked while Sue's cheery voice echoes through the phone.

"Ember dear, It's Sue! Will we still be expecting you for dinner?"

"Hi Sue, um, yeah." I clear my throat "Yes. " I turn away from his heavy gaze. "May I bring a friend?"

"That would be lovely! We'll see you around seven then dear."

"We have dinner plans?" Garret smiles as I hang up the phone.

"Sue and Charlie, the owners, invited us to eat Christmas eve dinner with them," I bite my lip. "Is that okay? Otherwise, I've got some packets of saltines in my purse and a bottle of water we could share." I look up at him as he pulls my bottom lip from my teeth.

"As appetizing as your meal of crackers and water sounds," his eyes dance with laughter, "maybe we should see what Sue and Charlie cook up."

"It could be squirrel." I wrinkle my nose.

"I've had squirrel, it's not half bad."

"Pfft!" I bat at his hand, "oh, you have not!"

"I have!" He follows me the two steps back into the seating area.

"When," I turn around with my hands on my hips, "tell me one time the elusive Hayes family feasted on a tree rat!"

"Clearly you've not attended the Fur and Feast Gala, then." He bites down on his lip to keep his laugh from spilling out.

I narrow my eyes. "I can't tell if you're serious or not right now," I burst out with a laugh.

He holds up his hand and crosses his heart, "scouts honor, although, I wasn't a scout, do they cross their heart and hope to die sticking a needle in their eye?" he rambles, "Anyway, so that part, I don't know, but it was a real event, and I did go. Squirrel tasted like chicken, but not as chicken-y."

I blink up at him, "okay that was a lot to unpack. I'm just going to hope they have other options."

***

Ember Riley, answer your phone!!!!!!!!!

Ember!!!!!!!!!!!!!!

Ember!!!!!!!!!!!!!!!!!!!

Ember!!!!!!!!!!

OMG!!

Chill, I'm here. What's up?

What's up? Garrett Hayes just casually shows up 8 hours away at a cabin in the middle of woods that you happen to be snowed in at and you ask ME what's up? Dad said he saw him at Harpers Hardware and Garrett rushed out after hearing you were stranded. It's so romantic. I'm seriously swooning. Why do romantic things never happen to me? You're such a bitch.

Well, thanks for all that. but like I said we're just friends.

Just friends my big ass!

He does want more.............

I fucking told you! You lucky bitch! Spill the beans!

There are no beans. We drank cheap wine, he said he wanted more, we can't because I live in Boston. The end.

ember.......... :(

What aspen? It wouldn't work.

Okay.... but without the job now what's holding you in Boston?

Chapter Nine

Garrett

I listen to the sweet sounds of Ember humming to herself in the shower, willing my cock to go down and not picture her naked, wet, and covered in suds. Ugh! I scrub my hand over my face. I let the cheap booze do the talking and spoke too soon. Said too much, didn't say enough. I don't fuckin' know. What I do know is I'm still securely in the friend zone, and I can smell her peppermint body wash from here. I toss myself back on the bed.

"...baby, It's cold outside." Her voice rings out. Yes, firecracker, it is. But it's hot as hell in here. I'm in my own version of hell. It's like when Scrooge falls asleep, and the angels visit him, showing him what different versions of his life could be. Here's mine—my girl, wet and naked, just feet away while I play the role of the nice guy for goddamn decades.

"...............so nice and warm... Look out the window at that storm........."

How long can a man be expected to play the nice guy until he gives out? I mean, there's a time limit on that, right? Some kind of life expectancy? I should Google that. Surely, I'm not the only pitiful bastard who's been in this situation. Jesus, I've lost count of the number of times I've relived that one night at the party where we lost ourselves and just let go. She let me have just a little taste, and I ended up between her luscious thighs.

"...............My sister will be suspicious... Gosh, your lips look delicious-"

Her lips were delicious. "Almost done in there?" I yell.

"Yep, just a minute!" I hear the squeak of the old water pipes. Good lord, even the strongest man can only endure so much, I wipe the sweat that's accumulated on my brow.

"Sorry," she steps out wrapped up in a red fuzzy towel. "I didn't mean to take so long." My throat tightens as she tilts her head at me, and a droplet of water drips from her hair down the side of her neck and travels down between her breasts.

"Oh no!" Ember gasps, "You look flushed, are you sick from that awful wine Garrett?" She came to stand in front of me, one hand gripping the towel, a mere flimsy piece of red fabric separating her naked breasts from my mouth.

"Say something," her warm minty scent wafts over me, as her worried wide blue eyes search mine. "We can cancel and just stay in; I'll rub your back." Her chest presses against mine, as she stands between my thighs, and I blink back at her while my brain remains stunted.

"Garrett?"

"I need a shower," a huge breath whooshes from me as I stand and grab my bag heading to the bathroom.

"Okay, I hope I didn't use all the hot water," she calls after me.

"Not a problem, I'll stick to a cold one." I shut the door behind me.

***

"Well, isn't this lovely!" Sue Clearwater welcomes us into her home, essentially a slightly larger version than the one Ember and I are staying in.

"I'm so glad you were able to join Ember, Garrett. When she showed up on our doorstep, she was frozen to the bone. Oh," she clutches her chest. "Charlie and I were heartbroken for her! And on Christmas, no less!" tears spring to her eyes.

I glance down at Ember, whose cheeks have become a beautiful shade of pink as she bites down on her glossy bottom lip.

"Well!" Sue wipes a tear from the corner of her crinkled eye. "You're both here now. Please come in."

"Sue, let the kids in the door, for God's sake," a man, who I assume to be Charlie, comes walking into the foyer. He looks similar to the jolly old elf himself. "Here let me have your coats," he reaches out. "You kids want a pop? I've got some cold Sprecher root beer in the fridge."

"They're not children, Charles!" She scolds, "Break out the hard cider!" She gives us a wink. "Look at us fussing over you two."

"Well, we're very thankful you've invited us to share your meal," I place my hand at the small of Ember's back, guiding her into the dining room. I swear I see her shudder slightly at my touch.

"My gosh!" Ember gushes, "this is amazing!" The table is set from one end to the next with turkey, ham, stuffing, potatoes, and any other fixings you could imagine.

"Thankfully, I'd sent Charlie to the Jewel for everything we'd need for our feast for this evening before the storm hit. He took so long, he damn near gave me a heart attack," she glances over, raising a brow in his direction.

He chuckles, "I stopped at that new Wahlburgers place for a burger." He shrugs, "I never was one to turn down a good cheeseburger."

Chapter Ten

Ember

"Sue, you are an incredible cook, thank you." I moan taking a last bite of buttery mashed potatoes.

Garrett nods in agreement, taking another gulp of his hard cider.

"I hope you've saved room for pie!" she calls from the kitchen.

"Susie-Q is famous for her pies," Charlie boasts. "I saved a special spot right here," he pats his stomach causing her to giggle, as she comes in carrying two delicious looking desserts. They are an adorable couple. Throughout the meal, we learned that they met backpacking through Europe. Charlie was lost, searching for someone who spoke English, and as he put it, "like an angel she appeared." Eventually they decided to settle down themselves but wanted to be around other travelers and that's what led them to open Traveling Pines.

"You really outdid yourself, Sue," Garrett praises, "I've never tasted better."

"Oh, it was nothing really," she smiles. "It was my pleasure."

"Oh my God," I moan again. "This pie is to die for." I lick the whip cream off my bottom lip and glance up at Garrett whose eyes look heavily down at my mouth. He shifts in his seat before taking another large gulp of cider.

"You might want to slow down on the cider," I lean over and whisper close to his ear, "or I'm going to have to grab a sled to pull you back to the cabin."

He smirks, before leaning closer, his warm cinnamon breath heating my skin. "You may want to stop moaning and licking whipped cream off your lips if you want to stay in the friend zone." He arches a brow as my shocked eyes meet his.

"Oh! I forgot the whiskey truffles!" Sue pops up and races to the kitchen.

"Well, we're in for it now," Charlie chuckles. "She gets a few whiskey truffles in her and look out!"

"Oh, stop now," she giggles walking back into the room, "my girlfriends tested a few during our game of bridge and they're not as strong as I usually make them."

"You say that every year Susie-Q," he pops one in his mouth and his eyes widen, “and every year they still surprise me."

"Well, I have to try one of these,” I let the truffle melt across my tongue. "Wow!"

"I told you!" Charlie shouts as we all laugh.

***

I sip my cider and pop another truffle into my mouth and curl up onto the couch next to Garrett, his arm hugging me tightly as I snuggle in closer. My entire body feels more relaxed than it has in weeks, months, even.

"Okay, so tell us again," I ask Charlie, who stands in the center of the living room. He starts moving his hands around animatedly. "Panic had completely set in at this point. I stood there trying to communicate with the locals through an intricate dance of hand gestures and awkward charades."

Sue holds her sides in laughter, "it was not that bad!"

"It was! The locals just looked at me, puzzled, like I was some sort of alien. I couldn't find my hotel to save my life. I thought I was going to have to sleep under an olive tree!"

I tuck my head into Garretts side, stifling my laughter and feel him place a kiss on top of my head.

"And then," he glances over at Sue, "this golden-haired goddess appeared in front of me, her

voice tinkling like wind chimes, and said the three words I was dying to hear - 'are you lost?' "

Chapter Eleven

Garrett

"I thought you weren't much of a drinker?" I say as I help pull Ember's soft green sweater over her head and try to think of anything other than the fact that I'm alone in a cabin in the middle of woods, undressing the woman of my dreams. She slowly bends down and tugs off her leggings, her pale legs seeming to go on for days. I swallow the frog in my throat as she stands back up in only an emerald, green lace bra and panties. Her long flowing red hair cascades down her back in soft waves. Think of something else, I chant, anything else, politics, crying babies-

She reaches up and cups my cheeks in her hands, her plush breasts brushing against my chest. "Oh, so serious, Mr. Hayes. We had so much fun tonight, what do we do now?"

"Now you go to bed," I say as sternly as I can manage.

Ember sticks out her bottom lip in a pout and crosses her arms underneath her chest, pushing it out slightly. My resolve breaks, and I scan her body, the barely there lace hugging every delicious curve. My heart thrums in my chest as I place my hands in my pockets before I do anything stupid.

"That's no fun, and Santa won't come anyway," she sighs.

I tilt my head. "Why's that?"

She gives me a devilish grin and my mouth goes dry, "Well, I've been a very good girl this year, but he doesn't know where to find me."

This woman is killing me. Even God himself would give in. "Santa always knows," I look around desperately for her bag as my remaining resolve begins to crumble away. "Do you have any pajamas to sleep in?" I ask in an attempt to distract myself from the tempting sight before me.

"I'd rather sleep in this," she says coyly as she grabs my shirt and pulls me close. My cock jolts in my sweatpants, every muscle in my body straining with the effort to restrain itself.

"You're a very confusing woman Ember Riley," I mutter as I slip my shirt over my head and onto hers.

"Mmhhmm, it smells like you," she buries her nose in the collar.

"Let's get you in bed," I pull back the quilt.

"Can we cuddle?" she asks over her shoulder as she crawls in.

"I was going to sleep on the couch" I motion over to the piece of furniture that's about two feet too short for me to lay comfortably on.

"Noooo! Come cuddle," she pulls at my hand. "I'll be good. I promise. Ugh, I hate the wire in these stupid things!" I watch her thrash around for a minute until suddenly her bra goes flying over my shoulder. Fuck. Me. Now. The woman is topless. In nothing but a lacy scrap of panties and my tee shirt, her eyes glazed and a lazy smile she peeks over at me, "come cuddle, Garrett, I'm tired." I force a slow inhale through my nose and an equally slow exhale out my mouth willing my body to behave.

Under her watchful gaze, I yank down my gray sweats and toss them on the chair in the corner. Now we're both only in our underwear. This is not good. If she doesn't keep her hands to herself, I'm not sure how strong I can be. I mean I'm only human and she's, well, she's Ember.

I climb in behind her wrapping us both in the warm quilt. The crackle of the fire lights up the room casting a warm glow across the walls as I listen to her soft breaths.

"Thank you, Garrett."

"For what?" I brush a piece of hair behind her ear.

"For tonight, for being here. For everything." She sighs and her body relaxes, molding perfectly against mine. *Just as it should.*

"There's no place I'd rather be on Christmas eve." I lay a soft kiss on her temple. She curls up closer, pressing her body against mine, I will my cock to behave as I take in all the warmth she has to offer. Gently stroking hair until I hear her breaths even out, and she falls into a deep sleep.

Chapter Twelve

Ember

I wake feeling warm, safe, and with a slight headache. I'm instantly aware of Garretts body, pressed against the back of mine. I glance down remembering I'm wearing his shirt. Bits and pieces of last night sort through my brain. I definitely pushed the limits and blurred the lines. Those damned truffles!

His warm breath coasts down my neck sending shivers along my body. His strong arm is wrapped around my waist and his extremely hard, solid cock, is pressed firmly against my ass. I squeeze my eyes shut and try to suppress a groan.

He presses his lips to the shell of his ear with a deep chuckle, "Little firecracker, if you keep squirming like that, we're going to have a problem." With a slight turn of my head, I look up into his eyes as they search mine. His lips are inches away, and I can feel the thunder of his heart matching mine. His soft pink tongue, that I know full well holds so much talent, peeks out sliding across his bottom lip, and my thighs clench in response.

My lips tremble as they meet his, in the faintest kiss. My head becomes light as he kisses me tenderly, brushing his tongue over the seam of my lips. He slides his body on top of me, with a groan that rubbles from his chest, his kiss instantly becomes intense. Deep. Dominating.

Our tongues collide, as I wrap my legs around his waist. His large warm hands caress across my skin. They're everywhere, gripping my thighs, pulling me closer, tangling in my hair. A tidal wave of emotions wash over me; my head spins and a warmth spreads throughout my veins. He kisses down my neck, sucking, biting, leaving goosebumps in his wake.

There is an undeniable hunger in his eyes as he moves his hands across my skin. I can feel the heat radiating off our meshed bodies as he sweeps his shirt up, exposing more of me - is this really happening? I pull it over my head baring myself for him, anxious to be touched. I can feel the wetness between my legs. I'm desperate for him, achy.

He gropes my breasts, grazing his thumb over my hardened nipples, erect with anticipation. Garrett grins smugly at my response as I arch my back and then his warm hot mouth sucks and flicks at my flesh. I grind myself against his cock, only my thin lace and his boxers separate us. He pulls my leg tightly around his waist and grinds his cock against my clit, while his hands skirt around the edges of my panties, the tips of his fingers just barely pulling at the edges.

"Just touch me," I whine breathlessly, arching impatiently against his hand. I can't make either of us wait any longer. Slowly, he slips his hand between my legs. A hushed moan catches in my throat when he finds my clit, massaging me in slow, precise circles. I cry out against his lips, "God, yes. Keep going." He does it again, this time his fingertip slipping lower and gathering my wetness. Teasing my entrance with slippery fingers, he exhales a sharp breath, "Fuck, firecracker," he whispers, dipping his finger inside of me. "Such a wet girl." "Yes," I moan arching my back, and pressing my breasts against his chest. He adds in another finger, and curls them, stroking my g-spot. Every nerve ending is on edge.

"I want to taste you so badly, baby girl. You have no idea how many times since that night-"

"Please," I desperately moan.

He pulls back hooded warm brown eyes searching mine, "yes?"

I nod, biting my lip, slipping my panties down my legs, and tossing them to the floor. Without my panties, my pussy is completely bare, swollen and glistening with my excitement. My breath comes out in short, shallow bursts.

He chuckles, "My girl is eager." He places soft wet kisses across the softness of my belly as he

makes his way down, parting my legs with a deep groan.

That feeling of the first swipe of his tongue almost sends me spiraling straight into an orgasm. It's this slow burning ache that starts at my toes, slowly building like a lightning bolt, coursing down my spine until it becomes a slow molten burn in my belly. I grip the back of his head and hold him tightly against me. Opening myself wide for him. Garrett's mouth surrounds my clit, sucking so hard it causes me to buck off the bed until his strong arms hold me firmly down. He eats my pussy as if he can't get enough, all the while groaning and lapping at my tender skin, telling me how good I taste. The slick, smacking sounds of Garrett's mouth against my wet pussy, the hushed sounds of his moans drive me wild. The way his strong arms hold my thighs open, the sensation of his wet tongue lapping at my clit, the feeling of my skin as it tingles with each swipe of his tongue.

He slides two thick fingers inside, curling up deep inside of me and just as the tingles down my spine start to become explosive, he backs off placing warm wet kisses down my thighs.

"No! Please, please don't tease me." I gasp, trembling with need.

"Don't worry firecracker," he looks at me with pure lust in his eyes, "I didn't come all this way to only eat this pussy once. I plan on making a meal out of you until we leave." He kisses back up my leg, running his tongue through my tender flesh.

"Yes," I eagerly moan, "please"

“Your sounds," he sucks, "your desperate little cries are my downfall.” He licks. "That's it, squirt all over my hand." It's his words that do it, my body shatters into pure bliss as my orgasm claims me. I see flashes of light; puffs of white smoke dot the edges in my vision. Sounds are muffled, but it's the blood rushing in my ears that drowns out all else.

Chapter Thirteen

Garrett

"Merry Christmas," I whisper into Ember's ear as I hold her tightly, running my hands down the soft skin of her back.

"MMerryChhss" she mumbles incoherently into my chest, coming down from her bliss. I chuckle into her hair. I'm surprised we haven't gotten a phone call to keep the noise down. My girl doesn't hold back. Although even if they could hear us, I'm certain Sue and Charlie would be happy for us. Before we left their home last night, Charlie pulled me aside and gave me a man-to-man pep talk.

The women had busy giggling over truffles and cider while we had a couple of cigars on the porch. He'd asked me about Ember and my story, and I'd explained a bit. "Well, boy, all I can say is, I see the look in your eyes when you look at her. It's the same way I look at my wife. Don't let her slip away. You'll regret it."

If only it were that easy. I'd left deciding that I would take whatever she gave me, and this morning that's what I'd done.

I wish I could go back and re-do the past three years. I should have been stronger when she left, fighting for her, and supporting her dreams. But at the same time, I didn't want to be a man who kept someone from making their own choice. In the end, I all but gave up.

The only times I did reach out was when I had too much to drink and the loneliness became unbearable.

I try not to be naive, but I can't help but feel like being here in this cabin, isolated amidst the snow-covered landscape, is like an alternate reality. When our stay here is over, I fear that I'll have to go back to living a life without her, and my heart can't bear the thought of it.

"Have you looked by the fireplace? Because Santa came," I grin against her soft red hair, inhaling her sweet peppermint scent.

"Funny," she looks up at me. Eyes still glazed over, hair looking freshly fucked.

I nod to the fireplace, "take a look for yourself."

Her eyes narrow as she sits up wrapping herself in the sheet and wiggles down to end to the end of the bed. I hear a slight gasp and then a small giggle that makes my heartbeat faster.

She peeks at me over one shoulder. "What's that?" Her eyes light up with excitement.

I shrug, "how should I know? He must have snuck in while we were sleeping. God knows I wouldn't have heard a thing over your snoring."

"I do not snore!" She tosses a pillow in my direction, and I duck while she scrambles off the bed scooting to the living area.

I slide on my sweats and take a spot on the love seat while she sits eagerly on the floor still wrapped in nothing but the sheet from the bed. If I remember one thing from this, it will be of Ember wrapped in a crisp, white sheet, her soft curves visible beneath its folds, the taste of her still on my tongue, while she looks at me excitedly waiting to see what "Santa" brought her.

Last night after she'd fallen asleep, I had ventured out alone to gather a pine branch from outside the cabin for a makeshift Christmas tree. That was about the best I could do for a Christmas tree in the middle of the night on Christmas eve.

"I love it" she touches the pine, with a giggle.

"Open your gift" I motion towards the small gift bag I'd placed underneath.

"Garrett" she gushes, pulling out the items one by one. Her face lights up when she pulls out one item at a time—bath salts, face masks, and lotions—all from her favorite bath and body

store.

It wasn't much, but on the drive here, I'd stopped quickly and grabbed a few items I thought she'd like.

"This is amazing," tears glimmering in her eyes as she settles into my lap, leaning into me. "So sweet," she whispers, her lips meeting mine.

CHAPTER FOURTEEN

EMBER

"Would you like to use this with me?" I ask shyly, peeking up at him through my lashes holding up the brown sugar bubble bath.

"What do you think?" His voice is low and raspy as he nibbles on my ear lobe, sucking it into his mouth and making me all wet and achy again.

I moan, leaning my head back as he moves down my neck, "and after, maybe we could binge watch some tv." His thumb brushes across my nipple, "oh God, and drink cocoa and then eat the goodies Sue sent us home with?" I gasp, as he switches to my other breast and pinches my hardened nub.

He chuckles, "whatever you want today, firecracker."

***

I swirl the sweet sugary smelling suds around with my hand, while I watch Garrett slide his boxers down over his firm ass and muscular thighs. I've decided to push all thoughts of responsibilities and rules I've set for myself aside and just fully enjoy the day. After all, It's Christmas, and I'm stranded alone in a cabin in the woods with one of my best friends, who also looks like an adonis and gives amazing orgasms. And it would be a shame to not make use of this amazing bathtub.

"You have devilish glint in your eye;" he chuckles as he slides in opposite me.

"Do I?" I smirk, my arousal evident in the way my body shifts slightly closer to his.

"Yeah, you do," he teases, leaning back against the edge of the tub as the steam slowly envelops us in a cloud of delicious tension. I Grab the body wash next to me and slowly start pouring it all over the loofah sponge making a lather. I trail it slowly over my neck, down my arms, Garrett watches my every move intently. He swallows thickly as he watches me circle my breast. I bite down on my bottom lip while I take my hard nipple in my forefinger and thumb, rolling and pulling it as I moan. He shifts in the bath. I can only imagine how hard he is under all these suds. The thought alone makes me moan louder.

I lift one leg out of the water, placing it on the tub's edge. I gasp as Garrett's hands slide up my calf and over my thigh. My breathing becomes increasingly ragged as his fingers toy with me. His hands move further up my body, tracing patterns over my hips before he lifts me splashing water over the edge of the tub and placing me on his lap. I straddle him, our lips inches apart. I can feel his long, hard cock pressed against my abdomen. Our warm, wet, naked skin sliding against each other's. My breath hitches.

The warmth of his gaze makes my cheeks flush and tingles run down my spine. His fingers graze my jaw, then twine in my hair as his thumbs lightly caress my nipples. A low moan escapes my lips as I feel a wave of pleasure rush through me. He lays kisses down my neck, and then moves to my breasts, sucking, licking, kneading them with expert hands until I'm panting for breath. His mouth finds mine again as I grind myself against him, feeling the hard length of his erection beneath me. The pleasure builds within me until I think I will explode, and I'm a panting, whimpering mess and he releases my nipple with a satisfied groan. "I'm in love with your boobs," he murmurs.

He traces my bottom lip with his thumb. I feel desperation crawling up inside my core. That this will end, and I'll be alone again. A realization flashes through my brain that I've been working myself so hard every day that I don't have time to think of the loneliness that gnaws in my belly.

I do something I know I shouldn't, I'm too caught up in him, in us. In this moment. I raise up and fist his cock edging it at my entrance. "Ember—" he looks between us, my small hand gripping his swollen cock. "Condom, baby. I should—" "We—" He lifts his head as I rock my hips forward. "Are you sure?"

"I'm on the pill, and I want you." I gasp. My heart beats faster as I press my forehead to his, "I want to feel you."

Without hesitation he enters me, stretching me wide in the most exquisite way, while he claims my mouth again. Butter soft, his tongue tangles with mine, lazy and lulling. I claw at him, as though I can't get enough, as though this day is going to end too damn fast, because I know it is. My heart feels like it's cracking with every delicious thrust.

"Hey," he stills, pulling back, wiping a tear that's rolled down my cheek. "Am I hurting you?"

"No, please don't stop." I beg, swiveling my hips, wrapping my hands around him and running them through his thick hair.

"Relax, baby," he murmurs close to my lips. The way he says it, with safety and desire, turns my entire body into a fluid state. He grips my hips and pushes deeper, hitting that spot, making me moan. "That's it, baby." His voice is hot and sweet rolling over me like molten lava.

The heat of his body is like a furnace against my skin, and I feel myself melting into him. His hands are firm on my hips, gripping me tightly as he increases the intensity of his thrusts. My breaths come in shallow gasps, as I beg him to push harder, faster. He drives his body deeper into mine with each stroke, sending waves of pleasure cascading through me. My head spins and my vision blurs as he keeps pushing until I'm on the brink of ecstasy. “Look at me,” he commands softly, his lips brushing against my temple. His deep brown eyes are filled with desire, as I do as he asks. In an instant, all the colors of the world seemed to come crashing down around us and then everything dissolved into a starburst of white light.

Chapter Fifteen

Ember

"What is your favorite episode?" Garrett asks as we binge watch a season of Friends.

I swallow the bite of blueberry muffin from the basket of goodies that Sue sent over, "gosh, that's a hard question. Especially when you're distracting me." I giggle and squirm on his lap.

"I'm the distracting one?" he nuzzles his face into my chest. "You're sitting on my lap in nothing but this robe."

"You wouldn't let me get dressed!" I laugh as he tickles my sides.

"Why bother when I'll just have to peel your clothes off in another hour?" he nibbles on my earlobe while trailing his fingertips up my thigh, enlisting a moan.

The office theme song rings out from my cell phone.

"What's that?" he cocks his head to the side.

"Aspen," I reluctantly climb off his lap. "That's her special ringtone."

I grab my phone and open FaceTime to see my sister's face on the screen. "Hey sis."

"Hey, besides your quick text last night, I haven't heard from you. Are you doing okay? Having a good Christmas despite everything?"

"Yeah, yeah. Things are good." Garrett stands up, and I struggle to tear my eyes off his bare chest and the little happy trail that leads down to the edge of his gray sweats.

"So...... how's Garrett?" My eyes snap back to my sister who's giving me a knowing grin.

"Garrett is good." What else am I supposed to say? We fucked like rabbits, and if I have my way, we'll be doing it again as soon as I'm off the phone?

And then, Aspen being Aspen, asks the question that I've been trying not to think about. "When does your flight leave back to Boston?"

I glance over at Garrett, his muscles tense as he stokes the fire. "Noon tomorrow." I answer, feeling a wave of nausea running through me at the reminder.

"Oh," she studies my face for a moment. A sister knows, no matter what words are said or how you try your best to hide your feelings. She nods slowly before mustering up a weak smile. "Text me if you need me."

"Okay," I reply with a fake smile, determined to keep my emotions in check. "Tell mom and dad I said, 'I love them', and I'll call when I get back home."

I back over to the overstuffed loveseat, and Garrett turns towards me. His lips upturn in a slight smile, but his eyes say volumes and his body remains rigid. "Do I get a special ringtone?" he asks.

I glance up at him, "Program one in." Our fingers brush as I place my phone into his hands. A current of warm soothing energy shoots through me just like it always does when we touch. Tears prick the edges of my eyes, so I quickly turn away and watch the snowflakes drift lazily outside the window. I know that morning will come soon and take me far away from this place, back to my real life in Boston where I'll spend New Year's Eve all alone eating cannolis from Mike's Pastry

Shop, like I have the last two years. My former assistant forwarded me an email this morning, she's hoping we can work together again. There are companies similar to the one we worked for hiring throughout the east and southern coast. I'll give myself until January second to wallow and eat like shit, and then I'll get my act together, find a new job and start fresh. It'll be okay. It has to be.

Garrett hands me back my cellphone with a shrug. When I look down at it, I see that he had chosen the theme song from Friends as my new ringtone. I give him a nod but find myself unable to speak without my voice cracking. He sighs deeply before walking into the kitchen

and turning around to face me again. His voice is gentle, "Hey, there's still some daylight left. Get dressed - let's make the most of it."

***

The cold air nips at my cheeks as Garrett and I step outside into the winter wonderland around us. It really is quite beautiful with trees glistening around us, weighed down by the heaviness of the snow. It crunches beneath our boots; the only sounds are the occasional bird tweeting hello. I inhale the freshness so different than the thick smog I'm used to smelling.

Garrett scoops up a handful of snow and smirks mischievously at me. "Snowball fight?" His eyes glint with a playful challenge, and I can't resist the infectious energy radiating from him.

"Bring it on," I giggle, crouching down to gather my own ammunition. The cold crystals sting against my skin as I pack them together, readying myself for battle.

The first snowball sails through the air, and I duck just in time, feeling the rush of icy wind as it narrowly misses me. Laughter spills from both of us as we engage in a dance of dodging and throwing, the world around us reduced to the thrill of the moment.

I manage to land a direct hit on his shoulder, "You're going to pay for that!" he hollers, retaliating with a flurry of snowballs that have me spinning and weaving to avoid them. I'm breathless and having more fun than I can remember having in I don't know how long.

The world blurs with motion, and the crisp air fills with our laughter. He tackles me to the ground, and we land in a soft cushion of snow. My heart races, not just from the exertion, but from our closeness. The weight of his body pressing into mine.

His breath mingles with mine, visible puffs of warmth in the cold air. Our eyes lock, and time seems to stand still as a wave of something unspoken passes between us. Sadness, desperation, passion. Without a word, his lips find mine, and the cold of the snow contrasts with the warmth of his kiss.

The world fades away as we melt into each other, lost in the magic of the snow-covered moment. The taste of winter lingers on our lips, as he nuzzles his cold nose against mine, "let's go inside, I need you."

Chapter Sixteen

Garrett

The door to the cabin barely has time to shut before we are clawing at each other's clothing. We throw our clothes wildly about the room in a frenzy, until the only thing left between us is her delicate red lace panties. I kneel before her and slowly slide them down the curves of her legs, enjoying the sensation of the soft pale skin against my fingertips as I toss them towards my suitcase.

"Am I going to go home with any panties?" she giggles, arching her back and pushing her breasts towards me enticingly. Her blue eyes twinkle in the dim light and her hair cascades across her shoulders like a brilliant red waterfall.

I lift my gaze from her perfect curves and flash a devilish grin. "Not if I have anything to say about it," I growl before burying my face between her thighs. My tongue traces her wet lips as she moans and pulls at my hair. I can feel her legs getting weak, so I stand. My cock is so fucking hard it's almost painful, but I'm not done taking care of her. I love watching Ember lose control.

"Get on the bed for me, baby. And spread your legs." Her mouth is agape as she blinks up at me, full of lust. " Spread them wide."

I groan, fisting my cock as she does what I ask without hesitation. So pliable when we're naked. "That's my girl."

I run my hand slowly up her calves trailing my fingers on the inside of her thighs making her moan. I kiss my way from her chin to the valley between her breasts, avoiding her nipples. She arches her back, seeking some kind of relief. When her moans turn desperate, I kiss my way down her stomach and then part her with my thumbs and blow across her clit, while she groans.

"Please, Garrett. Don't stop, please" Ember mumbles as I drive her crazy.

"I'm dying to slide inside of you, feel your tight walls around me, milking my cock." I groan, kissing the skin right above her clit.

"Oh Fuck!" She holds onto my hair tightly with her other hand. "Your mouth is made of magic." I keep her legs pinned to the bed as I swipe my tongue in one long sweep from bottom to top. Her entire body jerks with the contact. I do it again. She moans loudly and lifts her hips, pressing my face into her soaking wet pussy. I don't even get to use my fingers before she comes. Her body shakes and convulses against mine as I lick up all that she offers, savoring the taste of her. I leave a path of wet kisses from her stomach to her mouth, settling between her thighs. She stills, her eyes fluttering as I press forward. I'm lost in her, mesmerized by Ember and this electrical current that runs between us. Grabbing her ass with one hand I shift my hips back and thrust hard. Ember gasps, and I'm instantly worried I've been too rough.

"Shit. Sorry, "I slow taking a deep breath. My forearms are shaking with restraint.

She reaches out to me, her small hand running along my jaw, "For what?"

"Not too hard?" I kiss her palm. She shakes her head and matches my kisses moving across my jaw to my ear and whispers, "Come on, Garrett." Her eyes flash, "Fuck me." Her words settle deep in my belly, sparking something within me. That's it. Any ounce of restraint I had left is gone. I pull out until only the head of my cock is still inside and then push back in, fast and deep. "Like this, firecracker?" I take her garbled response as a yes and do it again. Her head lolls back and forth, I try to fight off the orgasm threatening to overtake me. It's coming anyway, and I can't stop it. Ember wraps her legs tighter around my waist, and her nails dig into my shoulders as I pound into her relentlessly finally giving into the sensations coursing through me, I explode with a guttural moan.

Chapter Seventeen

Ember

A sickening feeling of dread washes over me before I open my eyes. I'm not even sure my eyes will open. Last night Garrett and I had the most mind-blowing sex of my life, we did it again, and again, and then he passed out next to me, and I listened to him softly snore next to me. I watched how his long lashes rested on his cheeks. I caressed the smooth lines of his back and watched his full bottom lip jut out into a small grin. And then I grabbed my phone to facetime my sister, locked myself in the bathroom and dialed just as the tears started to flow.

Aspen knew the moment she saw my face. She heard me whisper-sob about how It had been the most amazing weekend of my entire life. I told her that Garrett made me feel special, and we connected in a way I never had with a man.

And then she listened, without judgment, as I explained why I had to let him go.

I slide off the bed and silently grab the comfy clothes I'd set aside to travel in, before heading to the shower. My assistant forwarded me two more job prospects, so my plan is to look those over on the plane. One foot in front of the other. Sometimes putting yourself first means doing things that don't feel right to begin with. Change and growth is hard. This job loss has thrown me for a loop, but I need to get back in there and not let it get me down. My brain is going a million miles an hour, and I can't stop it no matter how hard I try. Arguing with myself, reminding myself as to all the reasons I need to get on that damned plane. I worked too hard, studied my ass off and am still paying off college debt, to put all that aside for a man that, Yes! He's wonderful, and sexy, and says all the right things, and plays my body like a well strung instrument. I let out a deep sigh. But we live hours and hours apart. It would never work.

I suds up my loofah with the sweet brown sugar body wash Garrett surprised me with. I can't believe that was just yesterday. I feel like this bubble we've been living in has been a dream. A small laugh escapes me, picturing our Charlie brown Christmas tree he set up. And then a sob breaks free. Fuck! Why does this have to be so hard? A simple trip home for the holidays has turned into this life altering weekend. I'll never be the same, I wipe a tear as it slides down my cheek, careful not to get soap in my eyes. No man has given me butterflies like Garrett does, made the effort he makes, given the orgasms he does. Jesus, I've never cum so hard in my life.

"Hey," his warm deep voice breaks through the steam filling the small space. "You started without me." He pulls open the curtain, stepping in. He's so gorgeous it hurts. It literally hurts to look at him. I sigh again. His deep golden eyes search mine, his brows furrowing as a tear rolls down my cheek. His lips thin. "Let me wash you," he takes the loofah and applies more soap, "turn around" he orders, placing a light kiss on my shoulder. Why does he have to make this so much harder? Why can't he be horrible or say things to make me hate him? Softly he washes my body clean, stopping to gently kiss my lips. When we step out, he dries me with just as much care. Soft, gentle, desperate.

"Garrett" I gasp as his nimble fingers slide between my legs and find my aching clit.

"We have time." He leads me to bed; I can't deny him.

He entangles our legs, bringing me closer. His lips brush mine, so delicately my head starts to spin. He kisses me with passion and longing that pulls at my heart. He explores every inch of me, as though he's saving it to memory. Garrett rolls onto me, pinning me beneath him, and kissing me with urgency. Slowly he reaches between us stroking his cock, I bite his lip. He groans into my mouth, rocking his hips forward. Positioning himself at my entrance, he pushes in the tip, teasingly. “Please,” I breathe against his lips. He sinks into me with one, long stroke. Wrapping my legs around his waist, I dig my heels in edging him deeper, feeling his cock fill me completely. Our eyes meet as he slowly moves within me, he kisses me tenderly. Pushing his fingers through mine, he puts my hands above my head. He trails his soft lips along my jaw, my hard nipples press firmly against his firm chest. I close my eyes as he sinks into me, again and again, and I hear his breathing quicken.

"Ember," his voice is deep, raspy, breathless, "look at me." I open my eyes.

One strong hand comes to stroke my jaw, my head becomes light. "This, right here, I know you feel it, baby," he nuzzles my nose with his, "this is more." And then he kisses me as we both find our release.

***

"Want some coffee before we head out? I think there's one of Sue's muffins left, we could share." Garrett asks as I pack up the last of my things.

"Sounds perfect." I swallow hard. I've already told myself after the tears I let go in the shower, that was all the crying I would allow. If I can make it through this, I can make it through anything.

"Charlie and Sue said to tell you we're welcome back anytime we want." He sets our coffees and muffin on the small table. "And that if we wanted to come back during the summer when the place is really hopping, we could get a weekend free. Apparently, Charlie water skis." He chuckles awkwardly and runs his hand through his hair. I hadn't gone with him when he returned the keys to our cabin. I knew I could only handle so many goodbyes today, and if I started the waterworks up again with Charlie and Sue I would be doomed.

"They're sweet." I sit and pick up the large mug of steaming deliciousness. "Mmm.. you put in just the right amount of cream, thank you." I avoid his gaze like I've been doing since we tore ourselves out of bed and got dressed. Somehow with clothes on, my boundaries seem a fraction easier to maintain. As long as I don't make eye contact-

"Listen, Ember." He starts and my stomach flips. "I'm just going to fucking say it."

"Garrett," I can feel the tears starting to form.

"No, damned it!" his voice rises. "If I don't say anything I'm going to regret it, and if I say the wrong thing, I'll hate myself. If, by some crazy miracle, I manage to say the right thing..." He scrubs his hands over his face in frustration.

"Come back with me to Silver Springs," he says firmly, slamming his coffee mug onto the counter. The contents sloshing over the sides.

"I can't do that," I whimper, shaking my head.

"Why the hell not?" He throws up his hands, "You have plenty of options!"

"Garrett, you're asking me to give up the life I've established and the dreams that I've made for myself!" I rise quickly and dump my coffee in the sink before spinning around to face him.

"You'll make a new life! Your degrees are good everywhere. You have options!"

"In Silver Springs?" Despair fills my voice. "What kind of opportunities am I going to find there versus a big city? You're not being realistic!"

He's silent for a long moment before finally speaking again. "So that's your answer then." His eyes search mine for something he can cling onto, but he finds nothing. My mind is set.

"Garrett," I whisper his name brokenly, "I have nothing there."

His shoulders sag as he clears his throat. "That's how you feel?" His voice is soft.

"No," I reply quietly as a sob breaks free seeing the pain etched across his face, "I mean career-wise. You know how I feel about you." I swipe the tears away. "I just can't. I'm sorry."

He exhales and nods slowly in understanding. "I had to try," he shrugs.

"I'm sorry," he cups my face, wiping away my tears before pressing a soft kiss against my forehead.

"It's okay," he says, though neither of us believed him. "It's just bad timing; it's never worked out for us."

Chapter Eighteen

Garrett

My hands shake as I place her suitcase in my trunk. I shot my shot, and I lost. I can't say I didn't try.

I lean against the car, taking one last look around before getting in. I wonder what it must feel like to be a man like Charlie? To have the woman of your dreams say, yes. Yes, to you. Yes, to spending every day with you and doing whatever it takes. Lucky bastard. I thought for a minute, there was a glimmer of hope. But my girl is stubborn. The things I love the most about her are the things that will keep us apart.

"You ready?" I plaster on a smile as I slide in the car and buckle up. And then I drive to the last place on earth I want to.

We get there just in time for Ember's bags to be checked. She's flustered, trying not to miss her flight. Her cheeks are red, and she won't meet my eyes. I stand back, my hands in my pockets, while I watch her pass through security. The lump in my throat seems to grow, and my heart feels like it's being ripped out as I watch Ember get smaller and smaller until she disappears around the corner.

I see the last few passengers boarding the plane and hear the announcement that the flight is ready for takeoff. I lean against the window pulling my phone from my pocket when it vibrates. It's Sutton. I'd texted her earlier, so she knew how things were panning out, and

I'm sure she's worried. She's sweet like that, but I'm so overwhelmed I'm tempted not to answer. Then I remind myself, my sister is the only family I've got who gives half a shit about me, so I open it.

I scrub a hand over my face, I guess I don't have much more to lose. I dial her number and wait, hearing the phone connect.

I whip my head around as the chorus starts-

"I'll be there for you

(When the rain starts to pour)

my feet start moving in the direction of the sound-

I'll be there for you

(Like I've been there before)

I desperately search around for any sign of her-

I'll be there for you

('Cause you're there for me too)"

My heart beats wildly in my chest as I spot her just as the music finishes playing. She's digging frantically through her bag.

"Ember!"

"I couldn't do it," tears stream down her face as I lift her into my arms hugging her tightly. "I don't know how we'll make it work, I don't know what I'm doing" she sobs into my chest."

"We'll figure it out. Ember, look at me" I lift her eyes to mine. "I just need to know you're mine." I press my forehead to hers, "We'll figure everything else out."

"I'm yours."

EPILOGUE

EMBER

"Ready?" A deep, husky voice brings goosebumps across my skin while strong arms envelop my waist, drawing me snugly against a solid, warm frame. It's the voice of the man who unexpectedly captured my heart—the one who reentered my life and completely altered every passing moment thereafter. Over the past year, he's transformed my life into the happiest it has ever been. "As ready as I'll ever be," I smile. He grins and tightens his hold.

All this time, I thought I wanted to work on my career, and spend more time doing what I loved. But when it came down to it, I realized that there's only one person that I want to share these dreams with—one man who will always be there for me, no matter where life takes us. Garrett Hayes is mine, and I am never letting him go. "U-Haul is ready to go." My eyes scan the empty apartment once more, and I know without a doubt, I'm ready. Even though a piece of me will always miss Boston, I'm excited to see what Nashville has to offer. And the fact that it's close enough so that Garrett and I can finally sleep in the same bed every night, while still pursuing our careers, makes everything even better.

“I'm ready,” I tell him with more certainty, rising on the tips of my toes to press my lips to his. His lips move over mine, his kisses turning hungry. Growling against my lips, he says, “If we weren't already on a time crunch, I’d lay you down right here, and use my tongue the way you like so much.” My thighs clench. "Don't torture me, we have a long drive." I whine.

"If you're good, we'll find a way," he waggles his brows and slaps my ass as we make our way out the door. I have no doubt he'll be true to his word.

When we started this long-distance relationship, neither of us knew the roadmap for success or how we'd navigate the time until we could be together again. All we knew was we were committed to making it work.

As I step into the U-haul after he opens the door for me, I smile, "Let's head home."

"Home," he whispers, leaning in. "Damn, I love hearing you say that," he murmurs, capturing my lips with his. "Say it again."

“I can’t wait to go home with you,” I reply, feeling butterflies in my belly. Sure, I'm scared, but this feels more right than anything ever has because being together with Garrett, no matter where we live... feels right.

Want to read more from L.M. Maretti?

In the realm of love, Jules had sworn off believing. Hearts shattered; relationships crumbled—those weren't meant for her. She'd found contentment in her life, finding completion within herself, unshackled by the need for a man. But fate weaves its threads in unexpected ways, leading her to Aidan Anders—a man younger in years but brimming with charm and talents that defy his age. His proposition catches her off guard, a curveball she never saw coming. Perhaps, just perhaps,

exploring what he offers wouldn't inflict the pain she'd come to know.

Aidan's life is easy and uncomplicated, just how he likes it. A thriving self-made businessman with casual relationships that don't get in the way of his goals. Until Jules strolls into the frame, her hair aflame like a beacon and her curves commanding his attention. The pull between them is undeniable, magnetic, a force that won't be ignored.

Get your FREE copy of Friends to Forever Here- https://dl.bookfunnel.com/uv654r0fzf

ALSO, BY L.M. MARETTI

Echoes of yesterday, a Silver Springs novel book one

Whispers of Her, a Silver Springs novel book two

Since Forever, an Ander's brother's novel book one

Friends to Forever, an Ander's brother's novella

Cage of sin, a Toscani sister's novel

Reinventing the stars, a Toscani sister's novel

Dark

Obsession

www.ingramcontent.com/pod-product-compliance
Lightning Source LLC
LaVergne TN
LVHW040954150826
845672LV00002B/696

* 9 7 9 8 2 3 0 0 2 7 8 2 9 *